nickelodeon
TEENAGE MUTANT NINJA TURTLES

FOLLOW THE NINJA!

Adapted by Geof Smith
Based on the teleplay "Follow the Leader" by Eugene Son
Illustrated by Steve Lambe

A GOLDEN BOOK • NEW YORK

© 2015 Viacom International Inc. and Viacom Overseas Holdings C.V. All rights reserved.
Published in the United States by Golden Books, an imprint of Random House Children's Books,
a division of Random House LLC, 1745 Broadway, New York, NY 10019, and in Canada by Random
House of Canada Limited, Toronto, Penguin Random House Companies. Golden Books, A Golden
Book, A Little Golden Book, the G colophon, and the distinctive gold spine are registered
trademarks of Random House LLC. Nickelodeon, Teenage Mutant Ninja Turtles, and all related
titles, logos, and characters are trademarks of Viacom International Inc. and Viacom Overseas
Holdings C.V. Based on characters created by Peter Laird and Kevin Eastman.
T#: 312786
ISBN 978-0-553-51204-5
randomhousekids.com
Printed in the United States of America
10 9 8 7 6 5 4 3 2 1

The Teenage Mutant Ninja Turtles were on patrol. They had been looking for mutagen containers all night, but they hadn't found any.

"I'm so bored," Mikey whined.

"Let's take a break and do something fun,"
suggested Leo, the Turtles' leader.
"Awesome!" his brothers cheered.

"It's time for a training session!" Leo exclaimed.
"Aww," Raph, Donnie, and Mikey moaned. Ninja
exercises didn't sound like fun to them.

Leo had an idea to make training exciting. "We'll play King of the Mountain," he said, jumping to the top of Dragon Gate. "I'll stand up here, and you try to get past me using ninja skills."

"Sounds great," Raph said. He whispered a secret plan to Mikey and Donnie.

Mikey went first. He put on his headphones,
then flipped, spun, and danced right past Leo.
"Ninjas don't do that!" Leo protested.

Donnie calculated a sneaky way to throw his ninja stars. They bounced and skipped off buildings—right toward Leo.

Leo ducked, and when he looked up, Donnie was behind him.

Raph threw his *sai* straight at Leo.
As Leo dodged it, Raph jumped past him.
"That's not fair!" Leo shouted.

Leo was really mad. "You guys never take my orders seriously."

"Well, you always want us to fight just like you," Raph replied as he, Donnie, and Mikey marched away.

Back at the lair, Leo spoke to his teacher, Splinter. "Maybe I'm not cut out to be a leader," he said.

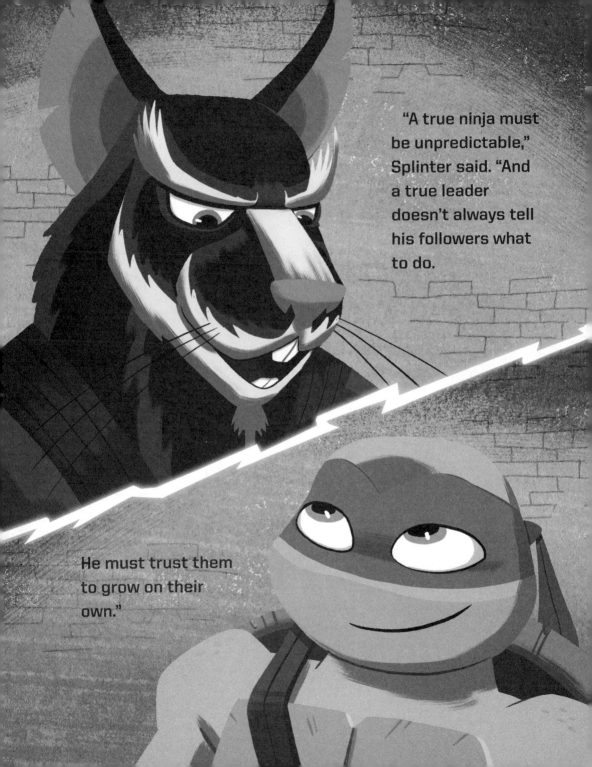

"A true ninja must be unpredictable," Splinter said. "And a true leader doesn't always tell his followers what to do.

He must trust them to grow on their own."

The next night, the Turtles went out again. Suddenly, Karai jumped from the shadows. She was a very dangerous ninja—and she wasn't alone. An army of ninja robots stood behind her!

"My Footbots are programmed to know every ninja move," she said. "You can't beat them!"

Karai commanded the Footbots to capture the Turtles. The bots charged, and the battle began. The Footbots ducked the Turtles' punches. They blocked the Turtles' kicks. The Turtles couldn't stop them!

Leo was sure the Turtles would lose this fight . . .
until he remembered Splinter's words: *A true ninja
must be unpredictable.*

"You can't program a ninja," Leo said. Then he yelled to his brothers. "Do you remember King of the Mountain? Show these bots your original ninja moves!"

The Footbots weren't programmed to deal with Mikey's dancing.
    Donnie was too sneaky for them.
    And Raph's power put the bots on the run!

$$\frac{b}{a+b}$$

"That's the most fun I've ever had following your orders!" Raph exclaimed.

"That's the most fun I've had giving them," Leo replied.

Mikey threw a smoke bomb,
and the Turtles vanished into
a purple cloud.

Back at their lair, the Turtles were ready to relax.

"Who wants to play King of the Mountain?" Leo joked.

"I'd rather play Follow the Leader," Raph said with a smile.